THIS WALKER BOOK BELONGS TO:

_____

_____

_____

_____

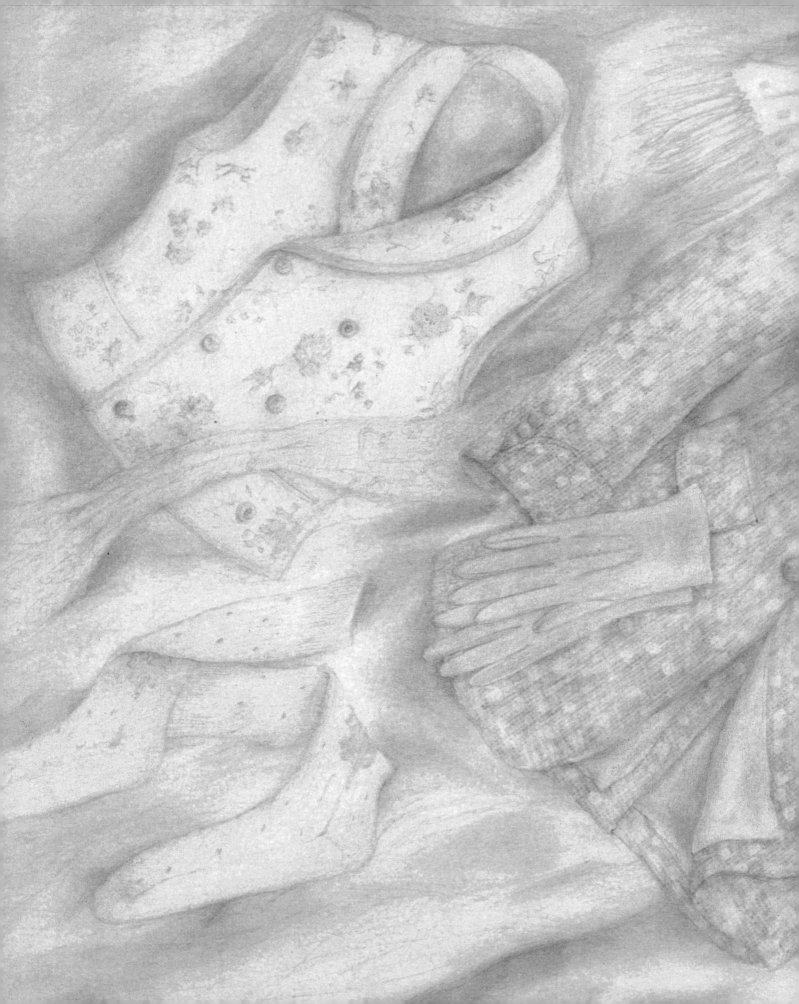

The Emperor's

For D.L. and L.I.
(the real magicians)

N.L.

First published 1997 by Walker Books Ltd
87 Vauxhall Walk, London SE11 5HJ

This edition published 2000

10 9 8 7 6 5 4 3 2 1

Text © 1997 Naomi Lewis
Illustrations © 1997 Angela Barrett

This book has been typeset in M Perpetua.

Printed in Hong Kong

British Library Cataloguing in Publication Data
A catalogue record for this book is available
from the British Library.

ISBN 0-7445-7295-9

New Clothes

by HANS CHRISTIAN
ANDERSEN

Translated
and introduced by

Naomi Lewis

Illustrated by

Angela Barrett

WALKER BOOKS
AND SUBSIDIARIES
LONDON • BOSTON • SYDNEY

FOREWORD

WHEN Andersen wrote this story, with its teasing end, he had no idea that — towards two centuries later — it would still be intriguing new young readers and listeners. The year was 1837. Andersen had been born to hardship and poverty. But even as a very poor boy (usually known as "the washer-woman's crazy son") he was an original, sure in himself that he would achieve a shining future. Now, as a young man, he had begun to make his way as a writer for adults: poems, plays, a travel book, a novel. Perhaps he had found at last the road that he was meant to follow.

But the special gift that he hardly knew he possessed had already started to show itself. Two years earlier, in 1835, he had, as a sideline, written four little stories, fairy tales of a sort, but not like any that people had known before. They were published together as a small book in the spring of that year. A booklet of three further tales appeared at Christmas. And in 1837 two new tales appeared. One was *The Little Mermaid*; the other, *The Emperor's New Clothes*. A wonderful pair!

Readers began to notice these unusual stories. A few wise friends of Andersen, who saw in them a rare strain of genius, encouraged him to write more.

Soon, in translation, the tales became known far beyond Denmark. The first English version appeared in 1846. We have been reading them ever since.

Andersen was to write greater stories than *The Emperor's New Clothes — The Snow Queen*, for instance. Yet this early tale, ninth in a total of one hundred and fifty-six, remains an obstinate favourite, certainly one of the most familiar.

Why is this? At first glance it could be just a traditional folk or fairy tale. Here is a monarch ruling a little kingdom, a simple fellow, you could say, but, by reason of his high position, not to be argued with by his smooth courtiers. There's a thread of magic, too; without belief, how could king and court *accept* the preposterous claim of the weaving cheats? Then, as in almost all fairy tales, no one has a name, just an allotted role, and that is that — or is it?

Not quite. Our emperor suddenly has to face an appalling situation. He steps out of his set role, and makes a heroic choice: he walks on. At once he is a proper monarch, a hero in his own right.

The saucy ending was daring enough in its day; it is daring still. But here is a curious fact. It was almost not there. In the original manuscript, already sent to the printers, these were the final words: "'I must put on that attire whenever I appear in a public procession or before a gathering of people,' said the emperor. And since nobody wished to seem stupid, everybody praised the wonderful new clothes." Not quite perfect, is it? Suddenly, Andersen saw how the tale should close. He rescued his copy and made the inspired change.

As a result, we have not only a funny story, but a wise one. How did the truth come home? From the piping voice of a child who hadn't learnt about accepted opinion. That is the real point of the story. Don't follow a way of behaviour, custom or tradition just because everyone else does the same.

In later days Andersen was often invited to read his stories in the courts of Europe. He was made a welcome guest by his royal hosts. But did he ever read them *The Emperor's New Clothes*? I wonder.

Angela Barrett's marvellous paintings in this book have a special interest. She has set the tale — a brilliant choice — at a time later than Andersen's own, yet still in many ways part of it: the final pre-war year of the little kingdoms that once made up Europe. That would be 1913. Early motor cars were on the roads — see the elegant Hispano Suiza; look very carefully and you'll find a biplane too. Yet people do not change. Tricksters, ministers, faces in the crowd, how real they are in the pictures.

Would Andersen have approved? Almost certainly yes. He lived from 1805 to 1875, a time of tremendous change and invention — from stage-coach to railway is one example. For Andersen, such practical new inventions stood for light and hope: they were a modern form of magic. No wonder he spoke of the future as "a time when fairy tales come true". Revealing words! Fact and fairy tale, each has its truth and Andersen makes them one. How could he not have enjoyed the pictures here?

The problem for illustrators of this tale is of course the final scene. Hundreds of different versions have been tried, bold or timorous. Original as always, Angela Barrett has provided one that carries full belief — and is like none other.

Naomi Lewis, 1996

MANY YEARS AGO there was an emperor, who loved fine clothes more than anything else in the world. Indeed, dressing up took all his time. Did he care to inspect his army? Or go to the theatre? Or ride out in his carriage among the people? Not at all – except as a chance to show off his latest splendid clothes. He had a different coat for every hour of the day. At times when you would be told of other monarchs, "He is in council", this emperor (if you asked) would be "in his dressing room".

LIFE WAS CHEERFUL anyway in the city. Strangers were always arriving, and one day a pair of shady characters turned up. Well, that's what they were, but they called themselves weavers. What's more, they declared that the cloth they wove was not only of marvellous beauty, but had magical properties: whether on the loom or made into clothes it was invisible to anyone who was unfit for his job, or particularly stupid. "Excellent!" thought the emperor. "Here's a real chance to find out which of my people aren't fit for the posts they hold – and I can sort out the wise from the fools. Yes! That stuff must be woven and made into clothes at once." And he gave the imposters a large sum of money so that they could start.

STRAIGHT AWAY
the rascally pair set up their
looms, and behaved as if they
were working hard. But, actually,
there was nothing on the looms at all.
Soon the men were demanding the
finest silk and golden thread; these they
crammed into their own pockets, and
just went on moving their arms,
as if they were weaving,
far into the night.

AFTER A TIME, the emperor thought, "I really *would* like to know how they are getting on." But when he remembered that the cloth could not be seen by anyone who was stupid or unfit for his work, he felt rather awkward about going himself. Of course he had no doubts about his own abilities – still, it might be a good idea to send someone else for a start. After all, everyone in the city had heard by now about the special powers of the cloth; everyone was longing to find out how stupid or incompetent his neighbours were.

"I know what I'll do," thought the emperor. "I'll send my honest old Chief Minister. He's the right man, as sensible as can be, and no one can complain about his work. Yes, that's the answer."

So the good old minister went along to the room where the false weavers were making a busy show of working at the looms. "Heaven help us!" thought the old man. "I can't see any cloth." However wide he opened his eyes, there was nothing. But he kept this to himself.

Then the two cheats begged him to step closer.

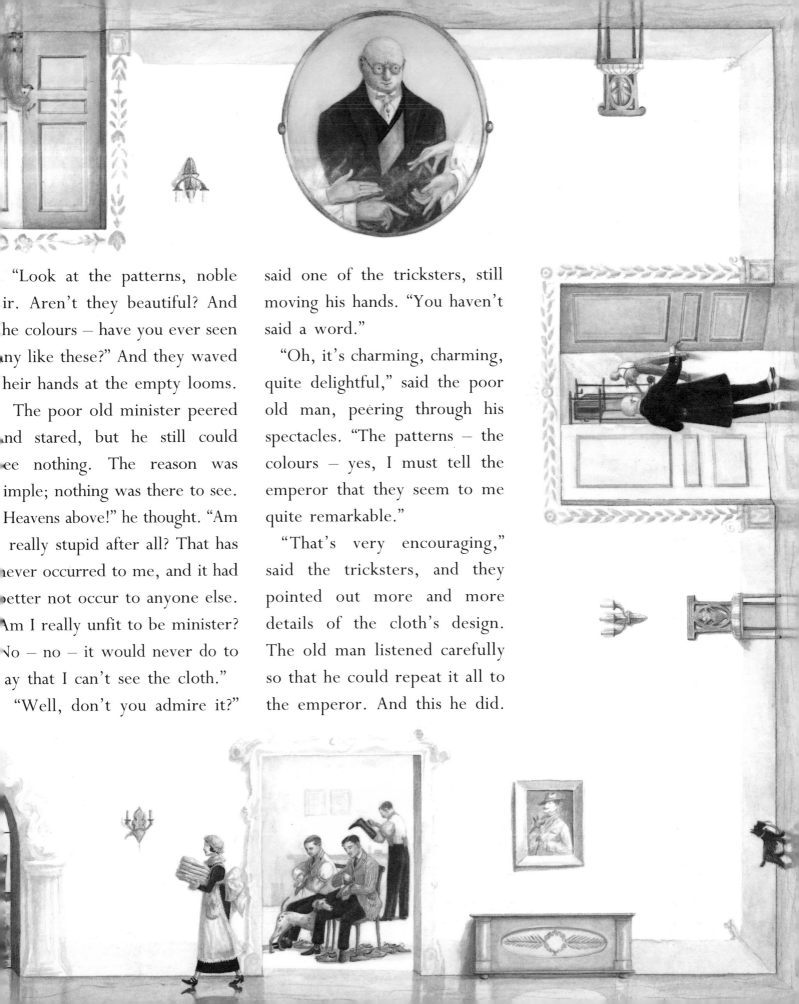

"Look at the patterns, noble sir. Aren't they beautiful? And the colours – have you ever seen any like these?" And they waved their hands at the empty looms.

The poor old minister peered and stared, but he still could see nothing. The reason was simple; nothing was there to see. "Heavens above!" he thought. "Am I really stupid after all? That has never occurred to me, and it had better not occur to anyone else. Am I really unfit to be minister? No – no – it would never do to say that I can't see the cloth."

"Well, don't you admire it?" said one of the tricksters, still moving his hands. "You haven't said a word."

"Oh, it's charming, charming, quite delightful," said the poor old man, peering through his spectacles. "The patterns – the colours – yes, I must tell the emperor that they seem to me quite remarkable."

"That's very encouraging," said the tricksters, and they pointed out more and more details of the cloth's design. The old man listened carefully so that he could repeat it all to the emperor. And this he did.

SOON THE ROGUES were demanding a further supply of money, silk and golden thread. They had to have it, they declared, to finish the cloth. But again, whatever they were given was promptly stuffed into their own

deep pockets. Of course, not a stitch of cloth appeared, though the cheats went on busily moving their hands at the empty looms.

Presently the emperor decided to send another honest official to see how the weaving was going on. "Ask how soon the stuff will be ready," the worthy man was told. But the same thing happened to him as to the minister. He looked and looked, but since there was nothing to see but empty looms, nothing was all he saw.

"Isn't it lovely?" said one of the rascals, and they lifted up the imaginary cloth and held it before the visitor. "See the designs, the colours." And they pointed out the beauties that did not exist.

"I don't believe I'm stupid," thought the official. "But maybe I'm not good enough at my work. Well, that has never before been questioned, and it had better not be questioned now." So he made admiring noises about the cloth he could not see. "Yes, yes, very handsome – splendid colours – superb design." And he reported to the emperor that the weaving was "magnificent!"

THE NEWS of the wonderful fabric soon ran through the city. At last the emperor made up his mind to look at it for himself. So, with the two who had already been, and a carefully chosen group of court attendants, he went to the weaving room. There were the two cheats acting about in front of the empty looms as busily as ever.

The two who had been before were the first to speak. "What splendid cloth!" said the old minister. And the other official murmured praise about the pattern and the colours.

As they spoke they pointed to the empty looms; they were sure that everyone else could see the lengths of stuff.

"This is terrible!" thought the

E

emperor. "I can't see a thing on the looms! Am I stupid? Am I unfit to be emperor? What a frightful notion! I mustn't let myself think of it – nor must anyone else." He then said aloud,

"Such charming material – charming!"

"Such charming material – charming! It has our highest approval." And he nodded in a satisfied way towards the empty looms. No one must guess that he saw nothing there at all.

The courtiers stared hard too, but not one of them saw a single thread of cloth. No wonder each of them secretly felt alarm. But, aloud, they echoed the emperor's words. "Charming!" "Charming!" They even advised the emperor to use the material for a new set

of robes to wear in the great procession that would soon be taking place. "It is magnificent – so unusual!" Every courtier felt obliged to murmur something

of the kind. And the emperor gave each of the swindlers an honourable decoration and the title of Imperial Court Official of the Loom.

New

er
the
unfit
frightf
myself
anyone e

'Such
mate
charn

ROR
SES
VER
AIR

ON THE EVE of the great procession the cheats were still at work on their imaginary task – the making of the clothes. All through the night they busied themselves by the light of at least sixteen candles. The outfit had to be finished in time. To the waiting courtiers the weavers seemed to be taking heavy folds of stuff from the loom; they seemed to be cutting, with big tailor's scissors, at something invisible; they seemed to be stitching away with needles that had no thread. At last they announced:

"The clothes are ready!"

And now the emperor made his way to the room with the most noble of his courtiers. At once the tricksters held up their arms as if they were lifting something. "Here is the jacket, your Imperial Highness. Here is the cloak." So they went on. "Their special quality is that they are light as gossamer. You might think from the feel that you were wearing nothing at all – but that makes them differ from all the usual heavy and cumbersome robes."

"Yes, indeed," said all the courtiers. But since there was nothing there to see, nothing was all they saw.

The rogues went on, "If your Imperial Highness will graciously take off the clothes you are wearing now, we shall have the honour of putting on the new ones here; you can see the effect yourself in the great mirror."

SO THE EMPEROR took off his
clothes, and the impudent pair
pretended to hand him the new
set, one thing at a time. Finally
they made a show of fastening on
his train. The imaginary costume
was complete.

The emperor turned and twisted
about in front of the glass. "How
elegant it looks!" "What a perfect
fit!" murmured the courtiers.
"What rich material!" "Such
splendid colours!" "Have you ever
seen more magnificent robes?"
No one would dare to admit that
he saw nothing.

"YOUR IMPERIAL HIGHNESS," said the Chief Master of Ceremonies, "the canopy waits outside." The canopy was to be carried over his head in the procession.

"Well," said the emperor, "I am ready. I agree with you that it is

really an excellent fit." Once again he turned this way and that,
for his final look at the mirror. The courtiers who were to carry the
train bent down as if to lift something from the floor. *They* were not
going to let people think that they saw nothing there.

SO THE EMPEROR walked forth in stately procession under the splendid canopy. People in the streets or at the windows called out such things as "Doesn't he look magnificent!" "Those new clothes! Aren't they marvellous!" "What elegance!" Can you wonder! For nobody dared admit that he or she couldn't see any clothes at all. That would have meant that the person was a stupid fool, or no good at his job. Indeed, not one of the emperor's gorgeous outfits had ever been so much praised.

Then, in a moment's silence, a child's puzzled voice was heard. "He's got nothing on!" "Shh!" said the child's father. "These little ones do talk nonsense."

BUT A WHISPER moved through the crowd. "A child over there says that the emperor has nothing on." "The emperor has nothing on!" Soon everyone was murmuring, "He has nothing on!" At last, the emperor himself began to think that they could be right. But then he thought: "If I stop it will spoil the procession. And that would never do." So on he stepped, even more proudly than before. As for the courtiers, they went on carrying a train that was not there at all.

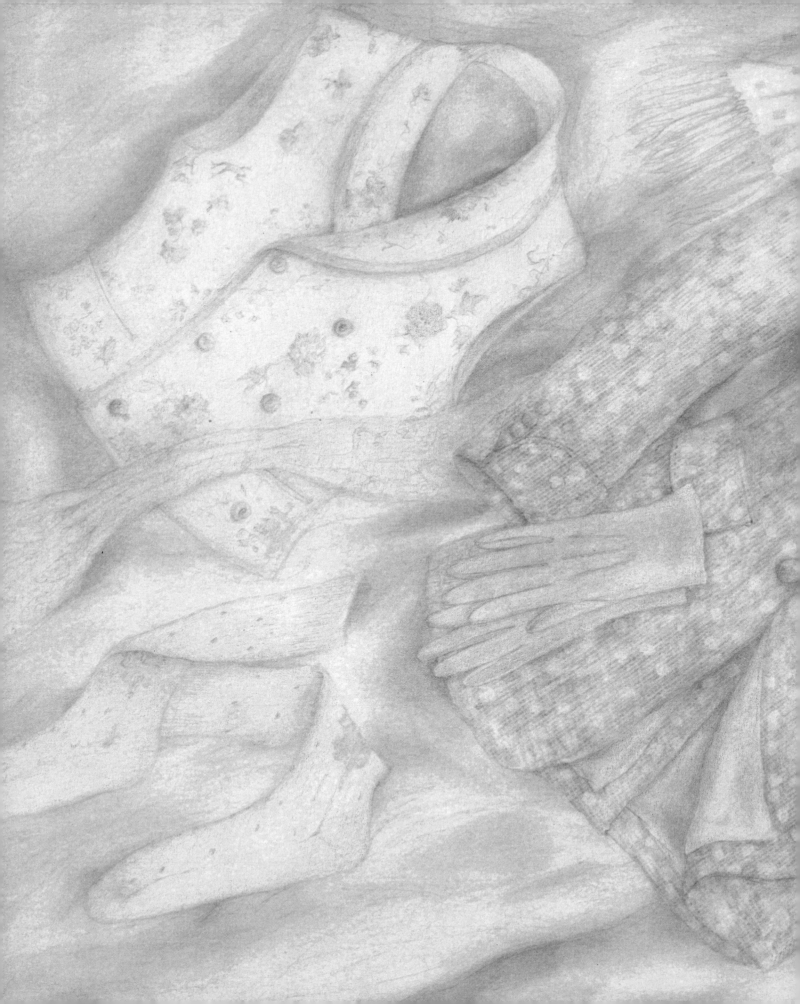

The Emperor's New Clothes

NAOMI LEWIS says one secret of the enduring popularity of *The Emperor's New Clothes* is that "humans don't greatly change, whatever the century. Look at the story here: the con-man rogues, the weak ministers, the plain-speaking child, the Emperor himself. The reader (that's you) will surely not find their behaviour odd or unbelievable. Of course," she adds, "Andersen was a rare original – no one before had written in his way or with such ideas. See too the introduction."

Naomi Lewis, poet and critic, is a leading authority on the work of Hans Christian Andersen. She first met his tales at the age of four and their magic has worked on her ever since. A Fellow of the Royal Society of Literature, she is a winner of the Eleanor Farjeon Award for distinguished services to children's literature. She lives in London.

ANGELA BARRETT has long had a fascination for fashion design and dressmaking, as is evident in her illustration of *The Emperor's New Clothes* – which is also notable for the numerous dogs. "They provide a commentary on the action," she remarks. Perhaps the most radical element of her interpretation, though, is her decision to make the child in the story a girl, "because I thought it was about time".

Angela Barrett won the Smarties Book Prize for *Can It Be True?* and the W H Smith Illustration Award for *The Hidden House*. She has three times been shortlisted for the Kurt Maschler Award and once for the Kate Greenaway Medal (for *Beware Beware*). Her other picture book titles include *The Walker Book of Ghost Stories* and another Andersen fairy tale translated by Naomi Lewis, *The Snow Queen*. She lives in London.

More Walker classic tales for you to enjoy

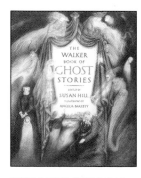

ISBN 0-7445-0766-9 (hb)

ISBN 0-7445-3298-1 (hb)

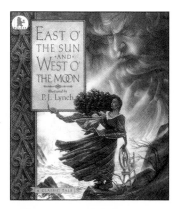

ISBN 0-7445-3166-7 (pb)

ISBN 0-7445-2005-3 (pb)